This edition published by Mantra Lingua Ltd,
Global House, 303 Ballards Lane, London N12 8NP, UK
www.mantralingua.com

からす王

かんこく民話

The Crow King

A Korean Folk Story

by Lee Joo-Hye
Illustrated by Han Byung-Ho
Retold in English by Enebor Attard

Japanese translation by Maiko Osada & Hideyuki Takemoto

むかしむかし、からすの　くにに　それはそれは　おそろしい　からすの
王さまが　いました。すきかってに　むらびとを　さらったりと
わるさばかり　していましたが、だれも　とめることが　できません。
あるひのこと、おとこと　おんなが　いえに　かえるとちゅう、とつぜん
からす王が　あらわれました。
からす王は　いっしゅんのうちに　おんなを　つれさり、にんげんが　いちども
あしを　ふみいれたことの　ない　たかい　とがった　やまへと
つれていって　しまいました。

A long time ago, in the land of the crows, there lived a king who ruled with terror.
He would take anyone he liked and no-one could stop him.
One day, a man and woman were going home when the Crow King came.
In one giant swoop he grabbed the woman and flew away to the steep and
lofty peaks where no human had ever been.

おとこは　やまが　どんなに　けわしく　くらくても、しろい　きりで
まえが　みえなくても　おんなを　すくいだすと　ちかいました。

The man swore that he would find the woman even though the land was rough
and gloomy, and he could barely see through the white mist.

おとこが　やまの　うえへ、うえへと　のぼっていくと　せんにんの
すむ　いえに　たどりつきました。
「それいじょうは　いかぬほうが　よい。」と　せんにんは
おとこに　ちゅうこくしました。
「いままで　おおくの　ものが　のぼろうと　した。」
おとこは　あいするものを　すくいに　いくのに　なにも
おそれるものは　ないと　いいました。
「わかものよ、ちからを　えるには　ゆうきが　ひつようじゃ。」
と　せんにんは　いいました。
「おんなの　もとに　いくまでに　１２の　とびらを
あけなくては　ならない。それぞれの　とびらで　からすたちが
おまえを　ころそうと　みはっておる。だが　おぼえておくがよい。
どんなことが　あろうとも　あくは　ほろびるのじゃ。」
そういって　せんにんは　わかものに　もちを　わたしました。
「さあ、からすたちの　きを　そらすのに　これを　もって
いくのじゃ。」

He climbed higher and higher until he came to a hut where a hermit lived.
"Go no further," she warned. "Many have tried before you."
The man said he was not frightened, for his love was true.
"Young man, you will need courage to be strong," the hermit said. "Twelve doors must you open to find her and at each door the crows watch, waiting to kill you! Remember, no matter what happens, even evil has an end." Then, bringing some rice cakes from her hut, she said, "Here, take these to trick the crows."

おおかぜが　ふき、　おおあめが　ふりました。あたりは　くらやみに
つつまれ　おとこは　そらが　おちてきたのだと　おもいました。
おとこは　やまみちを　いっぽずつ　のぼり　からすで　ふさがれた
１２のとびらの　とりでに　ようやく　たどりつきました。
からすたちは　とびまわり、　たべものを　つつきながら、
カーカーと　かんだかい　こえを　あげて　おとこを　みつめていました
むぼうで　おろかな　おとこだと　おもっていたのです。

The winds blew wilder, the rain fell harder. It was so dark that the man thought
the sky had fallen down. Step by step the man climbed until he saw the fortress
of a dozen doors with crows everywhere - flying, pecking, screeching,
watching - watching this foolish man ignore the danger ahead.

さいしょの　とびらで、おとこは　もってきた　もちを　からすたちに
みせると　とおくに　ほうりなげました。
からすたちは　おとこには　めもくれず　もちに　とびつきました。
そのあいだに　おとこは　こっそりと　にばんめの　とびらに　すすみました。
おとこは　こうして　すべての　とびらで　おなじように　もちを　ほうっては
からすたちの　きを　そらし　つぎの　とびらへと　すすみました。

At the first door the man showed the crows one rice cake and flung it far away.
The birds ignored him and rushed to the cake while the man quietly slipped through to the
second door. He did this over and over again and each time the crows ignored him.

じゅうにばんめの　とびらを　あけると　いっけんの　いえが　みずうみの
まんなかに　たっていました。
おとこが　おんなの　なまえを　よぶと、　おんなは　よろこびながら
おとこの　もとに　はしりより　だきつきました。
「いそいで。」と　おんなは　いいました。「おそろしい　からす王が
すぐに　もどってくるわ。」

Opening the twelfth door the man saw a house in the middle of a lake.
He called to the woman who rushed out and hugged him with joy.
"Hurry," she said, "the monster Crow King will be back very soon."

いえのなかには　りゅうの　かたちの　えのついた　きょだいな　かたな
と　くつが　おいてありました。
「はやく。」と　おんなが　いいました。「これらは　からす王のもの。
もっていきましょう。」
しかし、けんは　おもすぎて、くつは　おおきすぎます。
おんなは　みずうみの　みずを　つぼに　いれながら　さけびました。
「この　みずを　のめば　ちからが　つくわ。」

Inside was a huge sword with a dragon handle and a pair of shoes.
"Quick," she said, "these belong to the monster and you must take them."
But the sword was too heavy and the shoes were too big.
Filling a jug with water from the lake, the woman cried, "Drink this tonic,
it will give you courage."

おとこは　せんにんの　いったことばを　おもいだしながら　その　にがい　みずを
のみました。からだが　おおきく　そして　かるくなるのを　かんじました。おとこが
くつを　はくと　あしは　かろやかに　うごきました。かたなを　もちあげると　それは
まるで　たけのぼうのように　かるく、りゅうの　たましいが　からだの　なかに
はいってくるのを　かんじました。
もう　なにも　おそろしいことは　ありません。

The man recalled what the hermit said and drank the bitter liquid.
He could feel himself growing bigger and lighter. He put on the shoes
and his feet danced and kicked with ease. The sword he lifted was
as light as a bamboo branch and he felt the spirit of the dragon
enter his heart.
He was not afraid.

すぐに　からす王と　けらいの　からすたちが　かなきりごえを
あげながら　おしよせてきました。

They came a moment later. First the Crow King, then his follower crows, shrieking and spitting.

「きさま、このわしを　たおせると　おもっているのか？」　と　からす王は　いかりに
みちた　めで　おとこを　みつめながら　いいました。「おまえは　あまりに
ちっぽけすぎて　わしが　てを　くだすまでも　ない。」
からす王は　けらいの　からすたちに　むかって　いいました。「からすたちよ、
こいつを　ころせ。」

"So, you think you can kill me, do you?" said the Crow King, his eyes wild with anger. "You are too small and weak to bother with." Turning to his followers, he said, "Crows, kill him."

からすの　へいたいは　かたなを　かまえた　おとこに　むかっていきました。

The warrior crows hopped towards the man who swished his sword bravely.

おどろいたことに　おとこは　りゅうのように　たたかい、　からすの
へいたいを　つぎつぎと　ようしゃなく　たおしていきました。
ところが．．．

Then to their astonishment the man fought like a dragon,
killing them without mercy, until...

からす王が　やりを　もって　とっしんしてきました。
おとこは　うしろに　さがり、からす王の　こうげきを　かわしました。

the Crow King charged at him with a lance. The man leapt to block the charge.

おとこは　からす王の　ひだりうでを　きりおとし、つぎに
みぎうでを　きりおとしました。　しかし、　すぐに
あたらしい　うでが　はえてくるでは　ありませんか！

He cut off the Crow King's left arm, then his right arm.
But to his amazement they grew back immediately.

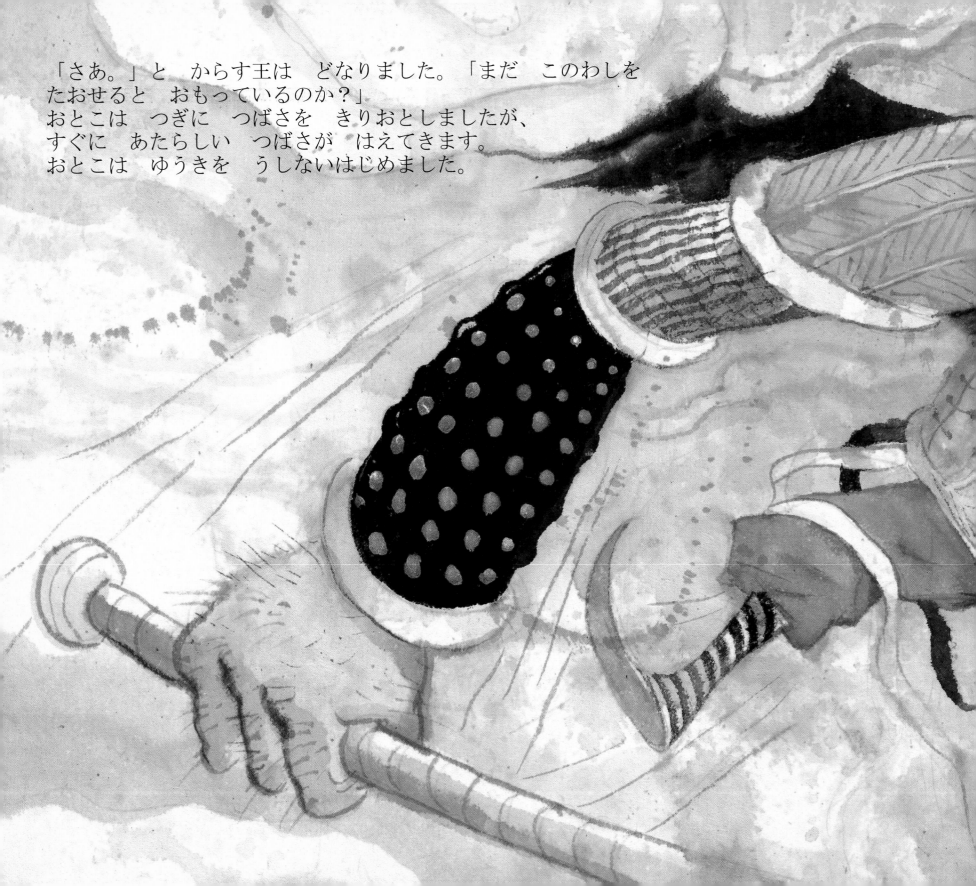

「さあ。」と　からす王は　どなりました。「まだ　このわしを
たおせると　おもっているのか？」
おとこは　つぎに　つばさを　きりおとしましたが、
すぐに　あたらしい　つばさが　はえてきます。
おとこは　ゆうきを　うしないはじめました。

"So," bellowed the Crow King, "do you still think you can kill me?"
The man chopped off a wing but when it grew back again his courage began to fade.

"His head," shouted the woman, quickly gathering a basket of ash. "No new head can be so evil."
And with a final swipe the man chopped off the Crow King's head. The other crows stopped
clawing, they stopped shrieking. For once there was silence everywhere.
The man and woman gathered the sword and shoes. They filled the jug with more water and left
the kingdom of crows, praying that a new gentler king would be found.

「あたまよ！」と　おんなが　はいを　あつめながら　いいました。
「うまれたての　あたまは　あくでは　ないわ。」　おとこは　こんしんの　ちからを
こめて　からす王の　あたまを　きりおとしました。
からすの　へいたいは　うごかなくなり、かなきりごえも　やみました。あたりは
しんと　しずまりかえりました。
おとこ　と　おんなは　かたな　と　くつを　にぎりしめました。ふたりは　つぼを
みずで　いっぱいにして　からすのくにを　さりました。こんどは　やさしい　王が
うまれることを　ねがいながら。